First published 2011 by Nosy Crow Ltd
The Crow's Nest, 14 Baden Place
Crosby Row, London SE1 1YW
www.nosycrow.com

This edition first published 2013

ISBN 978 0 85763 079 7

Nosy Crow and associated logos are trademarks and/or registered
trademarks of Nosy Crow Ltd
Text © Nosy Crow 2011
Illustration © Axel Scheffler 2011

The right of Axel Scheffler to be identified as the illustrator
of this work has been asserted.

A CIP catalogue record for this book is available from the British Library.

Printed in China

Papers used by Nosy Crow are made from wood grown in sustainable forests.

Pip and Posy

The Super Scooter

Axel Scheffler

nosy crow

Pip was riding on
his scooter.

He went **up** . . .

he went **down** . . .

he **even** did tricks on it.

Just then, Posy appeared.

Posy really liked Pip's scooter.

She wanted to ride on it a lot.

So Posy snatched the scooter and scooted away as fast as she could!

Pip felt **very** cross.

Posy had never been on a scooter before,
but she thought it looked quite easy.

She went up . . .

she went down . . .

. . . she even **tried** to do a trick on it.

Careful, Posy!

Then Posy fell off the scooter.

Oh dear!

Poor Posy!

She hurt her knee and was very sad.

So Pip looked after Posy and her sore leg.

"I'm sorry for taking your scooter, Pip," said Posy.

"Thank you for looking after me."

Pip and Posy had a **big hug**.

They went to play in the sand

where it was nice and soft.

And then they went
home for tea.

Hooray!